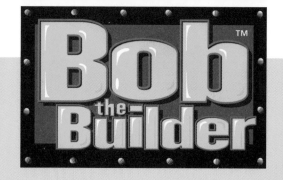

Bob the Builder™

Roley and the Rock Star

adapted by
Melissa Farrell

based on a book by
Diane Redmond

with thanks to
Hot Animation

SIMON SPOTLIGHT

New York   London   Toronto   Sydney   Singapore

Based upon the television series *Bob the Builder*™ created by HIT Entertainment PLC
and Keith Chapman, with thanks to HOT Animation, as seen on Nick Jr.®

SIMON SPOTLIGHT
An imprint of Simon & Schuster Children's Publishing Division
1230 Avenue of the Americas
New York, New York 10020

Manufactured in the United States of America

2 4 6 8 10 9 7 5 3 1

ISBN 0-689-85461-7

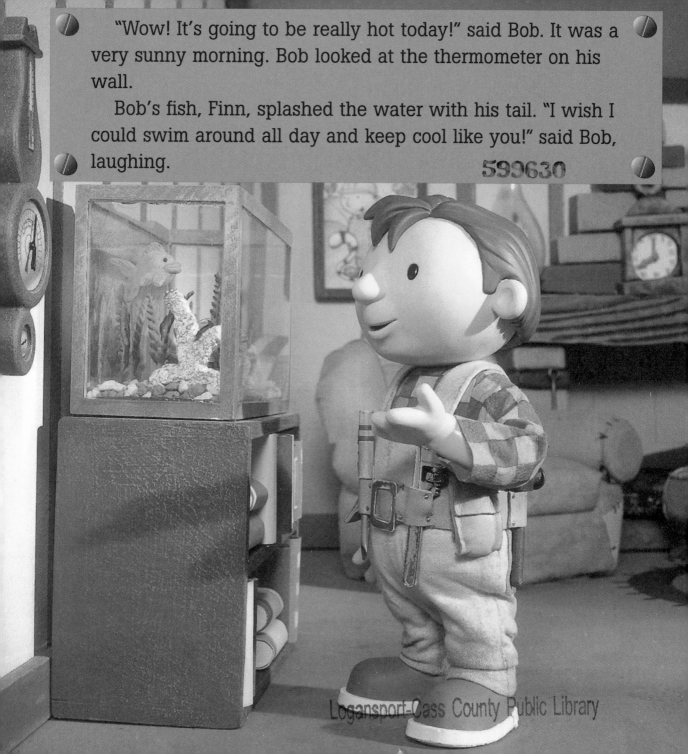

"Wow! It's going to be really hot today!" said Bob. It was a very sunny morning. Bob looked at the thermometer on his wall.

Bob's fish, Finn, splashed the water with his tail. "I wish I could swim around all day and keep cool like you!" said Bob, laughing.

Bob went out into the yard. "Morning, everyone! We've got two big jobs to do today," he told the machines.

"I've got to make a pond in Mr. Lazenby's backyard, and Wendy's laying out a nature trail in the park."

"Wow!" Roley rumbled. "Lennie Lazenby is the lead singer
of the Lazers. They're my favorite band!"
"Come on then, team. Let's go!" said Bob.

Wendy, Muck, and Lofty arrived at the park.

"This is where the nature trail will begin, so we'll need to put a signpost right here," said Wendy.

"What's a nature trail?" asked Muck.

"It's a path that people can follow to see all kinds of animals and plants," Wendy replied.

While Wendy and Muck were studying the map, a little duck suddenly popped out in front of Lofty.

"Quack," said the duck.

"Ooooh!" Lofty wailed.

"What's the matter, Lofty?" asked Wendy.

"A great big quacking thing just jumped out at me!" he cried.

"A duck?" asked Wendy. But the duck had hopped back into the bushes.

"I don't see any ducks. You must be dreaming, Lofty," said Muck.

Lofty kept a lookout for quacking things while
Muck and Wendy built a fence.

Just then two little ducks waddled up to Muck.

"Look! Ducks!" said Muck.

"Quack! Quack!" said the ducks.

Then another duck appeared on top of Lofty!

"Lofty, you were right," said Wendy. "Hello, little duck!"

"Ooooh, Wendy! Take it away!" Lofty yelled.

"You silly goose, Lofty," said Wendy. "The ducks are more frightened of you than you are of them! Come on, team, let's take them back to the water."

Meanwhile at Lennie Lazenby's house, Bob, Dizzy, and Roley could hear loud music.

"It makes me want to dance!" said Dizzy.

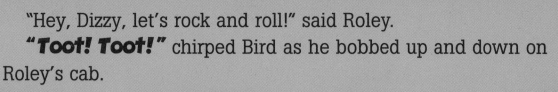

"Hey, Dizzy, let's rock and roll!" said Roley.

"Toot! Toot!" chirped Bird as he bobbed up and down on Roley's cab.

While Roley and Dizzy were dancing, Scoop dug a big hole for the pond, and Bob lined it with a waterproof sheet.

"I'll need lots of cement for the fountain next to the pond," Bob told Dizzy.

"Cement coming up!" said Dizzy.

Lennie Lazenby came out into the yard.

"Hello, Mr. Lazenby," said Bob.

"Oh, Lennie," said Roley, rushing up. "I really dig your music!"

"Cool! Maybe we should jam sometime," said Lennie.

"Wow! That would be great," said Roley.

"Isn't he cool?" Roley said as Lennie walked away.

"Yes, but he doesn't look like the kind of person who would make jam," said Bob.

"Ha, ha, ha!" laughed Roley. "Lennie doesn't make jam. Jamming is when people get together to play music!"

"Oh, *that* kind of jam," said Bob. "Silly me!"

Back at the park, Wendy found that the duck pond had dried up.

"Poor ducks. They must have been looking for a new home!" said Muck.

"Let's see if there's room for them at the pond that Bob is building for Lennie Lazenby," said Wendy.

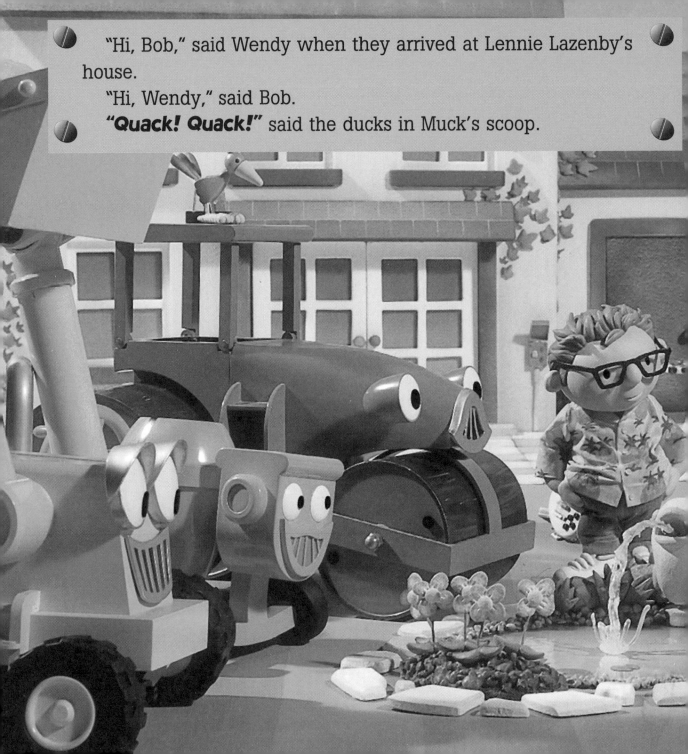

"Hi, Bob," said Wendy when they arrived at Lennie Lazenby's house.

"Hi, Wendy," said Bob.

"Quack! Quack!" said the ducks in Muck's scoop.

"Mr. Lazenby, the duck pond in the park has dried up," said
Wendy. "Do you think the ducks could stay in your pond?"
"Great idea! Ducks are, like, really groovy!" said Lennie.

"Aw, thanks, Lennie!" said Muck, gently sliding the ducks into the pond.

Everyone gathered around to see if the ducks liked their new home.

"Quack! Quack! Quack!" said the ducks as they happily splashed around in the water.

"Hey, let's celebrate!" said Lennie. "Should I sing my new single?"

"Yes, please! That would be cool!" exclaimed Roley.

Lennie started to play his electric guitar. Bob, Wendy, and all the machines danced around the yard to Lennie's music.

"Bob the Builder, can we fix it?" sang Bob.

"Bob the Builder, yes, we can!" Wendy sang back.

Soon all the machines joined in.

"Hey, groovy singing, Roley!" said Lennie. "Maybe you could sing on my next album."

"Wow! I'd love that," said Roley.